Published by Inhabit Media Inc.
www.inhabitmedia.com

Inhabit Media Inc. (Iqaluit) P.O. Box 11125, Iqaluit, Nunavut, X0A 1H0
(Toronto) 191 Eglinton Avenue East, Suite 310, Toronto, Ontario, M4P 1K1

Editors: Neil Christopher and Kelly Ward
Art Director: Danny Christopher

This project was made possible in part by the Government of Canada.

We acknowledge the support of the Canada Council for the Arts for our publishing program.

Printed in Canada

Library and Archives Canada Cataloguing in Publication

Title: When pumpkins fly / by Margaret Lawrence ; illustrated by Amanda Sandland and Margaret
   Lawrence.
Other titles: Paurngggaalualuittimmisippata. English
Names: Lawrence, Margaret (Educator and artist), author, illustrator. | Sandland, Amanda,
   illustrator.
Description: Translation of: Paurngggaalualuittimmisippata. | Translated from the Inuktitut.
   Original title transliterated from the Inuktitut syllabics.
Identifiers: Canadiana 20200259482 | ISBN 9781772272499 (hardcover)
Subjects: LCSH: Halloween—Nunavut—Sanikiluaq—Juvenile literature.
Classification: LCC GT4965 .L3913 2020 | DDC j394.264609719/52—dc23

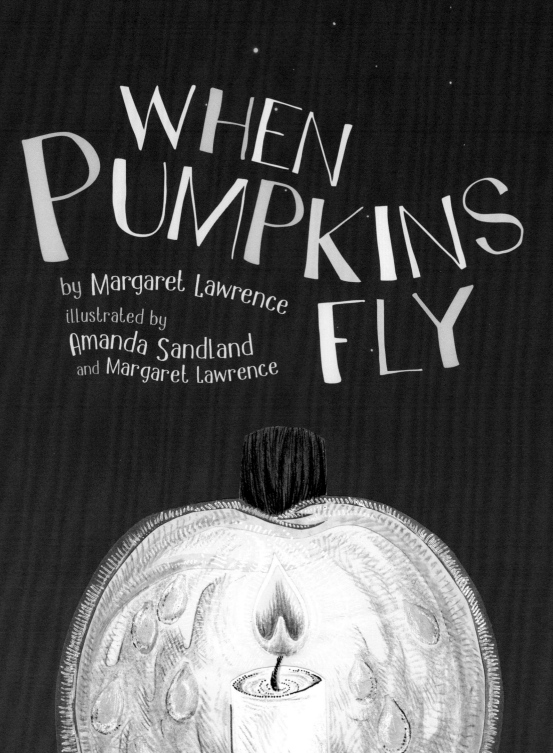

WHEN PUMPKINS FLY

by Margaret Lawrence

illustrated by
Amanda Sandland
and Margaret Lawrence

On the last cargo plane to fly into our community before Halloween, there are boxes, crates, and bags of groceries, snowmobile parts, and mail.

At the back of the cargo hold, there are also some passengers. They aren't wearing seatbelts to keep from rolling around because the seats have been taken out of the plane. The passengers are heavy, hard, cold—and orange!

This is the time of year when pumpkins fly!

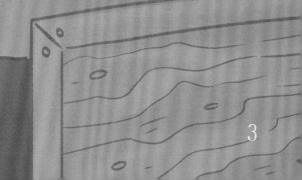

After the pilots land the plane and open the door, a truck pulls up. All of the cargo is loaded onto the truck. Soon a pilot closes the door, the engines start, and the plane flies away.

The cargo truck heads to the store before the groceries freeze. Our school principal has heard the plane fly overhead. She calls the store to speak with the manager.

"Please send some pumpkins to the school ASAP!" she says. That means "as soon as possible"!

When the pumpkins arrive, some older students help to bring a pumpkin to each of the classrooms.

I look at our big, orange guest. What kind of thing is a pumpkin? What are we going to do with it?

Some of you may already know about pumpkins. Each pumpkin is different. Will this pumpkin be funny, spooky, silly, or scary?

7

When school is almost over—after we have carved a face on the pumpkin, eaten raw pumpkin insides and baked pumpkin seeds, and cleaned up—the real excitement begins.

Someone will get to take the pumpkin home with them and put it on their porch for Halloween night! We get ready to pick a name from our teacher's mug, where we have put all of our names.

The teacher pulls out a slip of paper—and reads *my* name!

9

I carry the pumpkin home carefully and place it on my porch steps.

It gets dark soon after we get home from school. It's time to have tea and bannock and put on our boots, coats, and costumes.

Light the candle in the pumpkin! Tonight's the night for trick-or-treat fun!

There are kids, teens, Elders, parents with babies, and toddlers all out trick-or-treating. It's fun to go to every house. Our bags full of candy are heavy to carry when the wind is blowing hard.

13

When we've collected all we can carry, we go home for more tea. Maybe we'll have candy, pork chops, fish, or goose soup to eat.

We go to the community hall. There's a dance tonight for everybody, a costume parade, and a costume contest. There are games to join in, too.

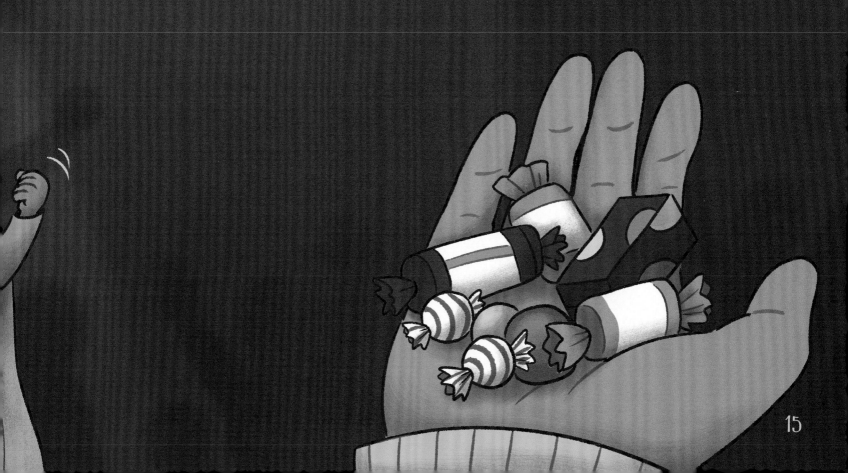

After all the fun, we go home. It's very late when we get to sleep.

As I drift off, I think about the *tunnaat* who live out on the land. Halloween is a night to think about these ancient and wise beings that like to visit our community.

When the night is dark, the tunnaat are awake. . . .

17

The wind blows harder and the candle in the pumpkin burns out. The pumpkin begins to change. It becomes wrinkled and shriveled. Then the pumpkin is frozen.

Maybe foxes and ravens will come to eat it? Or maybe snow will cover it?

When the tunnaat come to our community, they like to come at night.

They go into and out of houses, the store, the school, anywhere. They are looking for things they need. . . .

21

Maybe, just maybe, tunnaat will come tonight and carry the pumpkin away. Maybe tunnaat will take the old pumpkin with them, back out on the land.

But what will the tunnaat do with an old, old pumpkin?

Taima/The End

Until pumpkins fly again. . . .

23

Notes on Inuktitut Pronunciation

There are some sounds in Inuktitut that may be unfamiliar to English speakers. The pronunciations below convey those sounds in the following ways:

• A double vowel (e.g., aa, ee) lengthens the vowel sound.
• Capitalized letters denote the emphasis for each word.

| taima | TAI-ma | the end |
| tunnaat | tun-NAAT | Name for beings found around the community of Sanikiluaq. |

For more Inuktitut language resources, visit inhabitmedia.com/inuitnipingit.

Margaret Lawrence is an educator and artist. She was born in Japan and moved to the Canadian Arctic in 1980, first to Frobisher Bay (now Iqaluit) and then to Sanikiluaq in 1988, where she began teaching. She has spent more than half her life in the Canadian Arctic, seeing much change in the community over that time period. She has been fortunate to learn from four generations of Qikiqtarmiut, the people of the community she calls home.

Amanda Sandland is an illustrator living in the Toronto area. She studied illustration at Seneca College, eventually specializing in comic arts and character design. When not drawing, she can be found studying, designing characters, creating costumes and replica props, or burying her nose in a comic.

Inhabit Media Inc.
Iqaluit · Toronto